TOM PALMER

FOOTBALL ACADEMY

CAPTAIN FANTASTIC

Illustrated by
Brian Williamson

PUFFIN

PUFFIN BOOKS

Published by the Penguin Group
Penguin Books Ltd, 80 Strand, London WC2R ORL, England
Penguin Group (USA) Inc., 375 Hudson Street, New York, New York 10014, USA
Penguin Group (Canada), 90 Eglinton Avenue East, Suite 700, Toronto, Ontario, Canada M4P 2Y3
(a division of Pearson Penguin Canada Inc.)
Penguin Ireland, 25 St Stephen's Green, Dublin 2, Ireland (a division of Penguin Books Ltd)
Penguin Group (Australia), 250 Camberwell Road, Camberwell, Victoria 3124, Australia
(a division of Pearson Australia Group Pty Ltd)
Penguin Books India Pvt Ltd, 11 Community Centre, Panchsheel Park, New Delhi – 110 017, India
Penguin Group (NZ), 67 Apollo Drive, Rosedale, North Shore 0632, New Zealand
(a division of Pearson New Zealand Ltd)
Penguin Books (South Africa) (Pty) Ltd, 24 Sturdee Avenue, Rosebank,
Johannesburg 2196, South Africa

Penguin Books Ltd, Registered Offices: 80 Strand, London WC2R ORL, England

puffinbooks.com

First published 2009

015

Text copyright © Tom Palmer, 2010
Illustrations copyright © Brian Williamson, 2010
All rights reserved

The moral right of the author and illustrator has been asserted

Set in 14.5/21pt Baskerville MT
Typeset by Palimpsest Book Production Limited, Grangemouth, Stirlingshire
Made and printed in England by Clays Ltd, St Ives plc

British Library Cataloguing in Publication Data
A CIP catalogue record for this book is available from the British Library

ISBN: 978-0-141-32472-2

www.greenpenguin.co.uk

PUFFIN BOOKS

CAPTAIN FANTASTIC

ı Palmer is a football fan and a writer.
ıever did well at school. But once he got
reading about football – in newspapers,
ıazines and books – he decided he wanted
e a football writer more than anything. As
as the Football Academy series, he is the
or of the Football Detective series, also for
ı Books.

Tom lives in a Yorkshire town called
norden with his wife and daughter. The
stadium he's visited is Real Madrid's
iago Bernabéu.

Find out more about Tom on his website

tompalmer.co.uk

Books by Tom Palmer

Football Academy series:

BOYS UNITED
STRIKING OUT
THE REAL THING
READING THE GAME
FREE KICK
CAPTAIN FANTASTIC

For older readers

FOOTBALL DETECTIVE: FOUL PLAY
FOOTBALL DETECTIVE: DEAD BALL

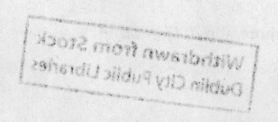

For James Nash and Sophie Hannah

Contents

The Best Team in Europe

The first game of the New Year was not going well. At least, not as well as the *previous* year had ended.

In December, just before the Christmas break, Premier League United's under-twelves had won a tournament in London, beating both Arsenal and Chelsea. And not long before that they had beaten Real Madrid. They had been written about as one of the best under-twelves teams in Europe. A crop of players that would go all the way.

But today they were at Tranmere Rovers. And they'd just let a third goal in.

Three–nil.

Ryan, the team captain, was furious. But not with his team-mates – with his mum.

She was on the sidelines shouting, like she often did. Arguing with the referee. Questioning the tactics of the under-twelves coach. Making Ryan feel embarrassed.

The referee blew his whistle for half-time as soon as the third goal was scored. And Ryan's mum went quiet.

Once the players had gathered on the touchline and were having their sports drinks, Steve, the under-twelves manager, started to speak. He was of medium height with dark hair and a deep voice.

'Right, lads,' he said, pausing. 'This is not going well.'

Ryan smiled. He liked his manager. He
knew he'd handle this properly.

'But don't worry too much,' Steve went
on. 'We've had a lot of changes since the last
game. Only Ryan is left from the defence we
played against Chelsea.'

Ryan dropped his head. He knew Steve
didn't mean to blame him. But he felt
responsible. He was captain, after all.

But Steve was right about changes in the
team. They'd lost their best defender, James,

who had decided to give up football. Their first-choice full-backs were still in Ireland, celebrating the New Year. And the stand-in left back was in a really bad mood.

Yet Ryan still felt responsible.

'We need the midfield to protect the defence more in the second half,' Steve said. 'Don't worry about getting this game back. Let's just keep it tight and try to win the second half. Yeah?'

Eleven lads nodded.

When they were back on the pitch, Ryan went round the players to fire them up. Especially Tony, who had replaced James in central defence.

Then Ryan went over to Craig. He was a big lad with wild hair and a ruddy face. He often played left midfield. Ryan knew that he had to handle this carefully. Craig had been difficult recently, as if something was troubling him.

'Keep it up, Craig,' he said. 'It's hard dropping back into defence, but you're doing a good job helping Tony out with that striker.'

Craig shrugged.

'Really, you are,' Ryan said. He was worried about Craig. He barely spoke these days, always angry and brooding.

Ryan patted Craig's back. 'You can handle this striker. I know you can.'

'I'll handle him, all right,' Craig said, grinning.

Ryan wasn't sure what Craig had meant. But once the game got started again, he didn't have time to think about it. The Tranmere forwards were all over them again.

And then Craig did what he had told Ryan he was going to do.

The Tackle

The next time the troublesome Tranmere striker got the ball he sprinted towards the United defence. He easily beat Tony, who just couldn't match his pace.

Then Craig ran at him.

Craig was a good player. He could play left back or left wing with ease. He could tackle and he had a lot of pace for a big lad. He wasn't a dirty player. Normally.

But as the striker pushed the ball into the

penalty area, Craig lunged at him. Two-footed. Making no attempt to reach the ball. Just the man.

It was a wild challenge. The striker went down hard. And he didn't roll about. He just lay there. Not moving.

Something was wrong.

And suddenly half the Tranmere team were pushing at Craig. Shoving him. Some United players got involved too: Sam and Daniel, two of Craig's mates. Craig ended up on the ground, looking up at the Tranmere players with a smile on his face.

If the referee and team coaches had not arrived then, things could have been worse. Much worse.

After the fighting, Ryan had noticed two things.

First, his mum clapping, as if she was pleased with Craig's tackle.

Then Steve talking to the Tranmere manager. Saying sorry.

Ryan was not surprised that when Craig stood up the referee showed him a red card.

Craig shrugged and walked off the pitch. Ryan saw Steve waiting for him on the touchline. He felt as low as he could remember feeling as a United player. They were losing three–nil. They were down to ten men. His mum was behaving badly. And he'd lost half his team-mates.

And now it was a penalty to Tranmere.

Tomasz, United's keeper, stood tall to put the Tranmere player off.

But it didn't work. Tranmere scored. Now United were four–nil down. And there were still forty minutes to go.

Ryan went round the team, trying to gee them up again. 'Come on. We can still get something out of this half. We can do it. Get one goal back.'

This was something he'd started doing recently. Earlier in the season he'd had a lot of trouble. With the other players. With Steve. He'd been – he had to be honest with himself – a bully. He'd been a bad captain. And Steve had stripped him of the captaincy.

But now Ryan was back as captain – and determined to do the right thing, to be a good leader.

Only he didn't feel like what he was

saying to his team-mates was true. He knew that today – whatever he said – they were going to get a sound beating.

The game ended six–nil. The worst result of the season.

As they came off the pitch, Ryan could hear the Tranmere parents cheering their team – and booing United.

And above those voices Ryan could hear his mum arguing with someone. He didn't want to look round. He wished she didn't come to watch him play. She was really embarrassing.

He saw Chi looking at him – like he felt sorry for him. And Tony, looking as if to say, *Can't you shut your mum up?*

And Ryan wondered if he could ever ask her just to stop coming. It had gone on long enough. Every week she became more and more unbearable.

Should he talk to her about it?

He wasn't sure.

Anyway, before that he had to talk to somebody else.

Sunday 8 January
Tranmere 6 United 0
Goals: none
Bookings: Daniel, Sam, Tony
Sendings off: Craig

Under-twelves manager's marks out of ten for each player:

Tomasz	4
Daniel	5
Tony	4
Ryan	7
Craig	2
Chi	6
Jake	5
Yunis	5
Sam	5
Ben	6
Will	5

Dressing Down

The United under-twelves walked back to the Tranmere dressing rooms in silence. Across a car park. Along a corridor. No one speaking. Everyone knowing that Steve was going to have something to say.

'Right, lads,' Steve said. But his voice was not what it usually was. Normally it was loud and clear. Today it was quiet and soft. 'We've played twenty or so games this season. Maybe twenty-five. And I've taken something

from all of them. Something good. But I'm struggling today.'

Everyone's head was down. Looking at the floor.

Then Steve said nothing for what seemed ages. It was like a minute's silence before a football match. As if someone had died.

During that minute Ryan thought about his mum. How she always shouted at the referee and the players. He wondered if his mum's behaviour was part of what Steve was talking about. Whether it was or not, he was determined to talk to Steve about her. Ryan knew he would be helpful.

'We were a few players light today.' Steve broke his silence. 'It's almost like the beginning of the season again. It took us a while to get used to each other then. New players. New ways of playing.'

A couple of the players looked up. Jake and Yunis. They had been new at the beginning of the season. They remembered how hard it was to settle in.

'But what I won't tolerate –' Steve's voice had grown louder, like it was normally – 'are tackles like that one, Craig.'

Ryan looked at Craig. He was staring back at Steve. His face looked neither happy nor sad. It was expressionless.

Nobody spoke. It was rare for Steve to pick on one of the lads in front of the others, for him to single the player out. It meant he was angry. Even though he wasn't showing it.

'I want to talk to you tomorrow, Craig. In my office. OK?'

Craig carried on staring at Steve. Then he shrugged.

Ryan saw Steve look away.

What is it with Craig? Ryan thought. *Why is he being like that?*

*

Ryan was one of the last to leave the dressing rooms. He had done it on purpose. He wanted most of his team-mates to be out of the way when he saw his mum. He knew she was going to be cross with him. She took any defeat really badly. So a six–nil rout meant she would not be happy. At all.

Ryan also wanted to talk to Steve. To apologize about his mum. And to find out what he was thinking about Craig.

Only Ben was left in the dressing room. He was looking at a newspaper.

'What are you reading?' Ryan asked. 'About United?'

Ryan and Ben both supported United's first team. United had been in the Premier League for years, but this season they were doing really badly. People were worried they might get relegated.

'Yeah.' Ben nodded.

'Is it about the manager? Has he been sacked?'

'Not yet,' Ben said. 'This is something about Neil Kelly's brother going to prison.'

'I heard about that,' Ryan said. 'What does it say?'

Ben shrugged and passed Ryan the newspaper.

Ryan read it out loud.

KELLY TELLS ALL

EXCLUSIVE *DAILY POST* INTERVIEW BY LIAM PRIESTLEY

It's raining at the United training grounds, and I'm here to meet Neil Kelly, United's talented left back.

Kelly is often in the news. For his famous hard-tackling no-nonsense play. For being the hard man of the team. For getting picked for England. For being part of a troubled United team this season, a team that could see themselves relegated. But today he's in the news for something completely different.

We are sitting in the players' cafe bar. Younger players from the junior teams steal a glance at Kelly as they walk past, perhaps wondering what this interview is for. Kelly brushes his hair away from his face. *He* knows what we're here to talk about.

His brother . . . who is in prison.

I ask him how he feels about it.

'Sad.' One word that sums it up. He offers nothing more.

There has been a lot of media coverage about

this part of Kelly's life. What does he think about the newspaper articles about his family?

'I regret it. This is a private family matter. It's very personal. But, because I can play football a bit, my brother is all over the papers.'

When I ask whether he misses him, Kelly is quiet. I can tell I've struck a nerve.

'I go to visit him. He's in an open prison, so it's not too hard to see him. But . . .' Kelly pauses. And I wonder if I've gone too far. 'But . . . I really miss him when we're playing at home. Since United signed me, he has had a season ticket near the players' tunnel. He always sits there. Then after the game we have a pint in the players' lounge. I miss all that.'

Kelly's brother will be going to prison for six months. I wonder whether this has affected his career. Is it hard for him to focus on the game? Does he feel let down?

'If you don't mind me saying so, that's a stupid question.' Kelly's got his hard-man face on now, the sensitive side of him gone.

But I'm only asking the questions the United fans want the answers to.

'My brother did what he did. He made a mistake. And he's being punished for it. Full stop.' Kelly is standing up now, putting on his jacket. 'He's not let me down. Maybe he's let himself down. But he's my brother. And I love him. And I think if I were to answer any more of your questions I'd be letting *him* down.'

And Neil Kelly leaves me on my own with the whooshing sound of the coffee machine. I think I upset him. The hard man of United didn't look so hard that afternoon in the United training complex.

'What do you think of that?' Ben asked, as Ryan handed the paper back to him.

'I think it's sad,' Ryan said.

'I meant the interviewer,' Ben said. 'Is he mean – or what?'

'Mean,' Ryan replied, as his friend walked to the door.

'See you later,' Ben said. 'Thanks for reading it out.'

'That's fine.'

The article puzzled Ryan. And then he started to feel nervous. With Ben gone it was time for Ryan to go and speak to Steve. About his mum.

Ryan's Problem

'Can I talk to you for a minute?' Ryan asked.

Steve sat down on one of the benches. 'Of course you can, Ryan. What's troubling you?'

'A few things,' Ryan replied.

Then Steve laughed. 'Me too,' he said. 'Me too. What a day!'

'I wanted to know what you thought of my mum,' Ryan said.

Steve was silent for a few seconds. Ryan

could tell he was thinking of the right thing to say.

'She's a bit loud, Ryan. But I don't expect you to do anything about it. It must be hard for you.'

Ryan just smiled and nodded.

'Shall I have a word with her?' Steve asked. 'Again.'

'If you like,' Ryan said.

'It's part of the whole agreement,' Steve went on. 'With you. With your parents. With your school.'

'I know. I read it in the Academy guidebook you gave us when I signed.'

Steve shifted on the bench. 'So, I'll talk to her?'

'Yes, please,' Ryan said.

'There's something else,' Steve said, 'that I wanted to talk to *you* about.'

Ryan wondered what it was. Maybe Steve

was thinking what he was thinking: that he wasn't a good captain because of all the trouble in the game.

'Don't look so worried,' Steve said.

Ryan sat up straight.

'I want to tell you how pleased I am with you,' Steve said. 'Since all the trouble we had in Poland, you have been great. You've really matured.'

Ryan tried not to grin too broadly. Praise from Steve made him feel good. Really good.

'You've been a fine captain. And a strong team member; I'm really proud of you.'

'Thanks,' Ryan said.

'But I can't say the same for your mother,' Steve said, smiling. 'I'll talk to her soon.'

Ryan nodded. 'And I was wondering about Craig. Do you think he's OK?'

Steve shook his head. 'He's been so different since the start of the London

tournament. I don't know what's got into him. Do you?'

'No. He won't talk.'

'Well, I'll have a word with him at tomorrow's training.'

'OK,' Ryan said. 'I've tried to talk to him. I'm sorry.'

'Sorry?' Steve said. 'It's not your fault.'

'But I'm the captain. I should be able to help.'

'Not with this, Ryan,' Steve said. 'You

are brilliant enough. Leave Craig – and your mum – to me.'

And Ryan wondered what Steve was going to do to Craig. He was behaving really badly, so he deserved whatever he got.

Ryan just hoped he didn't release Craig, make him leave the club. He'd never wish that on anyone.

But what *was* his problem?

Craig's Problem

Craig had left the pitch once he'd been sent off. He waited reluctantly for the post-match team talk, knowing he'd be in even more trouble if he left early. Even though he had somewhere to go. After the team talk he threw his clothes on and rushed to the nearest bus stop.

After a bus ride, he took a train. Two hours later he arrived.

It was two thirty in the afternoon when he got to where he was going. Tall walls. No windows. And bars. Lots of bars and gates and fences.

He'd never been in a prison before. Especially not to see his dad.

He was nervous. So nervous he thought he would be sick. But he had to do this.

Craig wouldn't have to go in alone. His dad's probation officer, Simon, was there too. They'd talked on the phone earlier in the week about the visit and made sure Craig knew what to expect.

Craig and Simon had to walk through some automatic doors that snapped shut quickly behind them. Then they went up to a counter, where three people sat facing them, unsmiling. Simon did the talking.

Next, they had to wait in a seated area, with several other families. Mostly women with their children. All the time watched by men dressed like police officers.

At every stage Craig felt more and more anxious. More and more like running away from this place. Simon had tried to talk to him, but Craig was so nervous that he didn't want to speak.

Then they had to leave their mobile phones and keys in a locker and walk through a scanner – like the ones at airports – before they were allowed into a room where several tables were set out.

Craig and Simon were told where to sit. They had one table. Other families were sitting at other tables.

Then a row of men filed into the room. All wearing the same-coloured clothes.

Craig's heart was beating fast.

Was he there?

What if he'd forgotten?

Or they hadn't told him?

What if he didn't see him until he was released?

He felt sick.

And then he saw his dad.

His dad was trying to smile. But not doing a very good job. He came across the room and sat down, leaning across the table to ruffle Craig's hair.

Simon pulled his chair away at an angle, trying to pretend he wasn't there, to give Craig and his dad some privacy.

'So how's the football? How's school?' his dad said. His voice was breathless. 'You look OK. Are you OK?'

'I'm fine, Dad,' Craig said.

'Good. Me too.'

'How's . . . How is it here?' Craig asked.

'Fine,' his dad said. Like he was staying in a hotel. Not a prison.

Craig didn't know what to say. He was used to talking to his dad in the car. Or in his front room. Alone. Not in a massive room. Not watched by prison officers. Not surrounded by families and noisy babies. Not with a probation officer sitting right next to them, pretending he wasn't there.

His dad smiled at him again. But it was a sad smile.

'We lost six–nil today,' Craig said to break the silence.

His dad shook his head. He looked genuinely shocked. 'What went wrong? Was Tomasz injured or something?'

'No. We've lost a few players. James has left. Ronan and Connor aren't back. Oh, and I got sent off for violent conduct.'

Craig's dad said nothing.

Then he spoke. 'Craig. I'm sorry I wasn't there. I'm sorry I'm never there.

I *was* thinking about you. At ten o'clock. I was thinking you'd be playing. I wanted to be there. So much. I miss you. You know that, don't you?'

Craig saw tears in his dad's eyes. One ran down his face.

Then Craig shrugged. He didn't feel like talking any more.

'Did your mum bring you?' Dad said.

Craig's mum and dad were divorced. They never spoke to each other. His mum had said she wanted nothing to do with Craig's dad. She refused to discuss it.

'No. She wouldn't come.'

'Right,' Dad said. 'I see.'

Then Craig's dad asked him about school. And they talked about football and how Craig was doing on *FIFA 10* and what books he was reading. Until half an hour was up and it was time to leave.

His dad hugged him. Tighter than
usual. And then he was called away with all
the other men. And Craig had to sit there
with Simon until they were told they could
leave.

Craig left the prison, after talking things
through with Simon. He wasn't aware of it,
but a man was watching him. A tall Asian
man in a posh coat.

Yunis's dad.

Craig walked out into the pale cold January afternoon, the sun already going down.

Ryan v His Mum

Sunday night.

Craig was home from the prison, upstairs in his room. And feeling miserable.

Less than a mile away, in an old stone terraced house, Ryan was in the kitchen, getting his mum a cup of tea.

He'd offered to make her one. He wanted to talk to her before Steve did and he thought this would be a good way to break the ice. Ryan carried the cup carefully into the sitting-room.

His mum had her back to him, the sofa set in the middle of the room, facing the TV.

Ryan's mum was on his PlayStation. *FIFA 10*. Ryan waited until the end of a game, when he knew there would be a pause between matches, before sitting down next to her.

'Here's your tea, Mum.'

'Thanks. Now tell me what you want.'

Ryan closed his eyes and smiled. His mum wasn't stupid. But this was not going to be one of their joke conversations. Where he asked for money for a new computer game or clothes. This could go wrong. Badly wrong.

'It's about the football.'

'Yeah?' Mum said.

'I'm worried,' Ryan said. He looked at his mum. She was looking at him, but she was miles away. In the middle of some *FIFA 10* fantasy.

'About?'

Ryan took a deep breath. The next game was ready to be played on screen. He'd nearly lost his mum's attention.

He knew he would have to be brutally honest.

'About you.'

'Me?'

Ryan's mum turned round. She'd put down her control pad. It had worked. He had her attention now.

'Yes.'

'What about me?'

'I want you to . . .' Ryan was struggling. 'I wish you'd –'

'What?' The word came out harsh and loud.

'Can you be less angry?' Ryan said. 'To the referees? To the other players? To Steve?' Ryan wanted to say could she be less angry with him, but he didn't dare go that far.

'Angry?' she shouted. 'You think I'm angry?'

'Like this,' Ryan said, wishing he'd never said anything. Wishing he was up in his room. Alone.

'Since when have you been worried about me being angry?' his mum said. 'I get involved. I come to every game. I support you.'

Ryan felt bad. Was she right? Shouldn't

he be grateful to her for being so interested?
He wasn't sure. He was confused.

And so he just sat there. Saying nothing.
Because that was what he did when his mum
got angry. It was like he'd been paralysed.
Like that insect he'd seen on TV: stung by a
wasp, its body was paralysed, but its mind still
working.

After a silence, his mum spoke in a
calm voice, a voice that worried Ryan more
than shouting. 'Did Steve put you up to
this?'

'No,' Ryan said. 'He asked me –'

'He what?'

'I mean . . . I asked him.'

'*You* asked *him*?' Mum was shouting
again.

Ryan went quiet. There was nothing he
could say. This could only get worse. Whether
he spoke or not.

His mum flicked NEW GAME on the screen before turning to Ryan for the last time.

'I'll go in and see Steve this week. I'll tell him what I think of him putting my son up against me. Don't you worry.'

Ryan got up and went back into the kitchen. He shut the door. Then he sat down at the kitchen table and put his head in his hands.

Steve's Problem

'Come in, Craig,' Steve said.
Craig edged round the door
and sat in the chair opposite Steve.
The office was small and filled with
footballs in bags and training cones. On a set
of shelves were stacks of box files and folders.

There was an hour to go before Monday
training kicked off.

Craig was glad to get in from the
car park. It was mayhem outside. Lots
of journalists waiting around, throwing

questions at anyone who walked by in a tracksuit.

'What's going on outside?' Craig said. He knew his voice sounded grumpy. He couldn't help it. But he thought it would be good to ask Steve a question, try and be a bit more friendly than he had been recently.

He knew he was in trouble.

'You've not heard?' Steve said, sounding grumpy himself. Like he was a man with problems.

'What?'

'They've sacked Flaubert.'

Craig was shocked by this news about the United first-team manager, but he said nothing.

'The board think United are in danger of going down.'

'We are,' Craig said.

Steve nodded and smiled. He liked to hear a football fan call his team *we*. Not *they*.

'What's going on, son?' Steve said, changing the subject. 'The last few weeks.'

Craig did a trademark shrug.

Steve smiled again. 'I need more than that, Craig,' he said. 'Your behaviour on and off the pitch is not good. It threatens you and it threatens the team.'

Craig didn't know what to say. He felt bad inside. Really bad. He'd still not got over how depressed the prison had made him feel.

He'd not even told his mum he'd been
there.

But he couldn't tell Steve about that.

'Do you remember when you signed for
United?' Steve asked.

'Yes.'

'Do you remember how you and your
dad signed this?' Steve pulled out a contract.

'Yes.'

Part of Craig wanted to say more. But he
felt like he was frozen inside. That he couldn't
say anything real to Steve.

'It talks about behaviour. How you
represent the club. How, if you make things
too hard for the coaching staff and the other
players, you could be asked to leave.'

Craig looked at Steve, saying nothing.
But he could feel his heart hammering in his
chest. So fast he felt sick.

'I'm not telling you that you have to leave,

Craig,' Steve said slowly. 'I'm asking you what's wrong. Is there something going on in your life that's making you like this?'

It was on the tip of Craig's tongue. He wanted to tell Steve about his dad. This was his chance. But he couldn't. Something was stopping him.

'Nothing,' he said quietly.

Steve nodded. 'If there ever is,' he said, 'then I am here.'

'OK,' Craig said. He wanted to leave. Now.

'I need to see an improvement in your conduct, Craig,' Steve said. 'Any more trouble and I'll have to bring you and your dad in here.'

Craig nodded, knowing that was impossible. How was he going to cope with everything that was happening to him? Especially without his dad there.

Defensive

'Right, lads,' Steve shouted. 'Today we're going to work on defence.'

Some of the players nodded. The team was still short on numbers. No James, no Connor and Ronan. But Craig was there, still worried by his chat with Steve an hour earlier.

The United training facilities were set in the estate of an old stately home. The playing fields were the grounds of the house. The offices and gyms were in the old stables.

It was a cold night. No cloud cover and

the stars were out. But the training pitch floodlights were on.

All the under-twelves were talking about the media in the car park. And the manager's sacking.

'I have an announcement before we start,' Steve said, catching their attention.

Craig felt his heart racing again. Maybe Steve was going to release him. In front of all the other lads. Use him as an example.

'Is it that Flaubert has been sacked?' Sam shouted out.

'No, Sam, that's not the news. But, yes, there's going to be a new United manager.'

'Are you leaving too?' asked Daniel.

Steve smiled. Then his face changed. To a frown.

'No, lads. Listen. I got a call from Ronan and Connor this morning. And – well, it's hard to say – but they've decided to stay at home. Not come back. It's been too tough on them, I think. Being over here, in a different country far away from most of their family and friends.'

There was a silence. Then voices.

'We'll be getting some new players in. Quickly,' Steve said. 'One of the new players will be Ben Hansford from the under-elevens. I think most of you know him. But for now we'll have to make do with you lot.'

Steve noticed Ryan had his hands on his hips. That he was looking at all his team-mates. Even though he was feeling sad about losing three players in a fortnight, Steve was pleased with Ryan. He'd changed. He wasn't thinking of himself. He was being a captain. A natural captain.

Training did not go well for Craig and Tony.

Steve had the team playing on half a pitch, with a full-sized goal at each end. Six players on each side short-passing. And with the pitch being so small, all the defenders and attackers were busy all the time. Especially as each time the ball went out of play a new one was thrown in. So there was no time for getting your breath back.

You had to be focused. And fit.

Craig and Tony's team lost. Heavily.

During the training session Craig had

been feeling more and more angry. Every time the forwards had beaten the defence he had taken it really personally. He was used to playing alongside James. James had rarely made mistakes.

But Tony?

He was useless. He was the reason the defence was so poor against Tranmere. The reason training had been such a shambles.

And to make things worse, Craig had

seen that almost every player had a parent on the touchline. He saw Ryan's mum. Jake's dad. Even Yunis's dad who, he remembered, never used to come to the football. And Tony's mum *and* dad were there.

'That was hard work,' Tony said to Craig.

Craig looked at Tony. He was tall but thin. Gangly. That's what Dad would have called him. But Craig kept his mouth shut. He knew if he spoke he'd start having a go. Tony was not a regular. Who was he to tell Craig things had been hard work?

'But we'll get it together,' Tony went on. That was it. Enough.

'*We?*' Craig said, stopping.

Tony turned round. But he said nothing. His face looked shocked.

'We?' Craig repeated.

'Yeah,' Tony said, keeping his voice low.

'It's not *we*,' Craig said. 'It's *you*. That's the problem. *You*. And you not being good enough to fill James's boots.'

But now he'd said it, Craig didn't feel any better.

He felt worse.

Yunis's Dad

Yunis's dad waited in the car park after training. He wasn't quite sure how to handle this.

Yunis had told him that Craig was behaving badly. Really badly. But Yunis's dad knew more than everyone else. Something he'd not even told his son.

He'd seen Craig with his dad inside the prison. Mr Khan was there because he was a solicitor and one of his clients was in that prison too. He'd thought about talking to

Steve. But then he didn't know if Steve knew that Craig's dad was in prison. And it was Craig's business. Not Steve's. So he decided he'd talk to Craig first.

Craig was out before any of his team-mates. He was still in his training kit, his jacket clutched in his hand. And he was walking fast.

'Craig?' Mr Khan saw him stop. 'Craig?'

Craig turned round and looked at Yunis's dad, who was walking towards him.

'How are you doing?' Mr Khan said.

'OK,' Craig said. He looked suspicious.

'I wanted to ask you something.'

Craig looked irritated. Mr Khan could imagine why.

'I wanted to talk to you about your dad.'

'What about him?'

Mr Khan chose his words carefully. Craig didn't sound like an eleven-year-old boy. He sounded different. He decided to be upfront.

'I work at the prison. I'm a solicitor. I saw you there. Yesterday.'

Mr Khan watched Craig's face cloud over. His face red and puffy. His eyes dropping to the floor. And then he started running. Away from the car park, down the long drive.

*

Yunis came out of the dressing rooms with
Jake and Tomasz. They were laughing.
Messing about. Like they didn't have
anything to worry about, Mr Khan thought
as he watched them.

Except that Yunis's face changed
when he saw Craig running off. Away from
his dad.

In Mr Khan's silver Mercedes Yunis
looked at his dad. His dad had just turned the

engine on and was ready to drive off, once his son had put on his seat-belt.

'What just happened with you and Craig?' Yunis said. 'Was he giving you grief? I told you he's been acting weird.'

'No, Yunis. It was something else.'

'What?'

'I'm not sure I can tell you.'

'Why not?'

Mr Khan cut the engine and turned to his son. 'Listen, Yunis . . .'

Yunis was surprised. His dad was nervous. His dad was never nervous. His dad was always in control.

'Do you know if there's anything going on with Craig? Maybe with his family?'

'Not that I've heard,' Yunis answered.

'Right.' Mr Khan paused. 'I don't know if I should talk to Steve.'

'What about?'

'This is between you and me. For now.'

'OK.'

'Craig's dad,' Mr Khan said. 'Well, he's in prison.'

Rubbish Parents

Training on the Wednesday had the same focus as two days before. Steve wanted to build the confidence of the defence and get them used to playing with each other.

Like on Monday, Steve had the rest of the team testing the new defenders in pairs. Using a six-a-side game on a short pitch.

Short-passing.

No time to rest.

Defence becoming attack. And vice versa.

And things went better than Monday. Ryan and Tony were working together more effectively. Daniel seemed to be coping with right back, having never played as a defender before. Even Craig was coping – and not shouting at people.

At the end Steve looked delighted.

'Well done, lads. That was great. Good defending, Tony, Craig, Ryan, Daniel. That sets us up nicely for Sunday's game.'

As always, all the boys made sure they were carrying something back from the training session. Ryan carried the bag of balls, which he always did, as captain; Tony, the corner flags; Tomasz, some cones.

As they walked across the fields, Yunis dropped back. He'd seen Craig walking slowly – and alone – at the rear and he wanted to talk to him.

Ryan was just ahead of them.

'Well played today, Craig,' Yunis said.

'Thanks,' Craig replied. Cagey.

Yunis hadn't quite worked out what he was going to say. He'd considered telling Steve about Craig's dad. But, like his own dad, he was worried Craig wouldn't want him to. So he decided he had to talk to Craig first.

And he also knew he had to be direct.

'My dad saw you at the prison,' he said.

'Yeah?' Craig said, in a way that made

Yunis think he should mind his own business.

'It can't be easy,' Yunis said, thinking straight away that he'd put his foot in it.

'Do you want another fight?' Craig said sharply.

'No,' Yunis answered. He was scared. He didn't want a fight with Craig. Not again, like they'd had earlier in the season. 'I want to ask if I can help.'

'Well, you can't.' Craig had stopped walking. He was shouting now. 'You and your dad – and his fancy car – can stay out of it. All right?'

'All right,' Yunis said. 'I will.' Craig scared him when he was like this.

But now Ryan was jogging back to them. 'What's going on?' he said.

Craig threw the cones he'd been carrying to the ground. His face was red with anger.

'What's going on is that both of you –' he

looked at Yunis and Ryan in turn – 'need to keep your noses out of my business. So what about my dad? Yours aren't much better. They're rubbish parents. Your dad couldn't be bothered to come and see you until weeks into the season. And as for your mum, Ryan, she's the worst parent I've ever seen. So there's no need to be so smug, is there?'

Straight Talking

After his rant, Craig ran off, leaving Ryan and Yunis standing speechless.

It was dark now. The floodlights that illuminated the training sessions had been switched off.

They walked slowly back along the path and over the small bridge that led to the dressing rooms.

'Let's give him time to get away,' Ryan said.

'Yeah,' Yunis agreed. He knew his dad

would be waiting for him in the car park. The last thing he wanted was for his dad to witness anything more like that. He might want to withdraw Yunis from United again.

Back in the dressing room all the other lads had gone home. Including Craig.

One of the showers was still on. Ryan switched it off. Then the two boys sat on the ring of wooden benches that went round the walls of the dressing room.

'What was all that about?' Ryan asked.

Yunis wondered if he should say anything. His dad had said it was a secret. But something had to be done about Craig. In fact, something had to be done *for* Craig.

'You know my dad's a solicitor?' Yunis said.

'Yeah.'

'Well, he saw Craig at one of the prisons he was visiting on Sunday.'

'What was Craig doing at a prison?'

'His dad's in there.'

Ryan put his head in his hands.

Yunis watched him. Had he been right to tell Ryan? He thought so. Ryan was different from how he'd been a few months ago. He'd been a bully, lording it over the other players. They'd even had a fight with each other. But now he was acting like a proper captain.

Ryan looked up eventually. 'Can I tell Steve?'

Yunis nodded. That was exactly what he thought Ryan should do.

Ryan waited until Yunis's dad's car had drawn away from the car park before he went to talk to Steve.

He saw his mum waiting in her car. She was playing on her PSP. He could see her, head down, face twitching, head jerking as she played whatever it was she was playing. *FIFA 10*, probably. And he realized that she'd not been to see Steve and that she probably wouldn't. She'd wait until she got angry during a match and do it in front of everyone.

He wondered if it was sad that his mum – aged forty-one – was into playing on a PSP. He wasn't sure. So long as none of his team-mates saw her.

Ryan knocked on Steve's office door.

No answer.

He knocked again. And then he heard
Steve's voice coming from the main entrance.

'I'll get fish and chips, love,' Steve was
saying.

Ryan walked to the doorway. Steve was
on the phone. He was starting to have second
thoughts about telling their team manager.

'Yes, love,' Steve said. 'Ten minutes. I've
just got to grab some stuff. Hang on. I'll come

now. I've to be here tomorrow afternoon anyway. From midday to six. There's some kit being delivered.'

That was it. Steve was in a hurry. Ryan wouldn't tell him now.

Ryan slung his bag over his shoulder, said goodnight to Steve and headed over to his mum's car.

He had a lot on his mind.

Three players had left.

One was in trouble. Big trouble.

And they'd lost their last match six–nil.

There was a lot to think about. He wasn't quite sure which way he should turn.

Chi's Advice

When they got home, Ryan's mum put on Sky Sports News straight away.

'Make us a cup of tea, will you, Ryan?' she said.

Ryan went into the kitchen and put the kettle on. Then he joined his mum in the sitting-room and sat down, half listening to the TV.

Rumours abound at United this evening about who will replace their sacked manager. Favourites are the

former coach of Milan, Primo Pavarotti; the current
Leeds manager, Howard Revie; and the existing
assistant manager, Martyn Bedford.

Whoever it is has quite a job on their hands.
United are in grave danger of relegation and club
morale is at a record low. We talked to some fans
about how they feel . . .

For once Ryan was too worried about
something that wasn't just football-related
to pay any attention to speculation about
United. Normally he'd be glued to the TV.
But tonight he was thinking about his own
team. The team he was supposed to be
captain of.

He wished his mum was like, say, Jake's
dad. Someone you could talk to, take your
problems to. But she'd just go off on one
and probably create more trouble than there
already was.

Sky Sports News was now talking about something else. He saw an image of the United player Neil Kelly, talking to his brother who famously sat in the stand every home game to support him.

And then it clicked.

He had an idea. Something that could help Craig. And therefore help United.

But first he had to talk to someone. If it wasn't going to be his mum, it would have to be someone else. Someone wise and calm. Someone he could trust.

Ryan picked up the phone and dialled. The phone rang four times. Then a voice at the other end.

'Hi, Ryan.' Chi's voice. 'Everything OK?'

'Chi. I need to ask you something.'

'Sure,' said Chi. 'About training tonight? It was better, do you think?'

'Yeah,' Ryan said. 'But it's not about that.'

'Right,' said Chi.

'There's this thing happening at United . . .'

'Craig?'

'How did you know?' Ryan was surprised Chi had hit the nail on the head.

'I've seen it all going on. What's the problem?'

Ryan told Chi what he knew. About Craig's dad being in prison. And Neil Kelly's brother being in prison. And all the trouble

Craig was making for himself – and that there was no one to help him. And the idea he'd just had.

'It's a good plan,' Chi said, 'but you have to tell Steve straight away. It might just work out.'

Media Scrum

Later the next day Ryan walked up the long driveway to the United training facilities, glancing into cars to see if he could spot first-team players, even though he knew they'd all have gone home after lunch. They only trained in the mornings.

But something was different today. There were a lot of cars on the drive. More than usual.

Ryan felt good about what he'd decided to do.

At the top of the drive, near the dressing rooms and the other buildings, Ryan saw a few vans. Some had satellite dishes on top of them. Most had the logos of TV or radio stations. And there were several people standing around with cameras, microphones and notebooks.

Ryan assumed that United had appointed a new manager, and that the media were here to report on it. If there was ever a big game – or a big story – at United, both the stadium

and the training ground would be besieged by the TV, radio and newspapers.

He looked into Steve's office as he made his way through the media scrum. And there he saw something he didn't expect.

Steve was sitting at one side of his desk, Ben at the other.

Ryan decided to leave them to it.

While he was waiting round the corner from Steve's office, Ryan overheard two football reporters chatting. They were saying that Martyn Bedford had been appointed as the new team manager. Ryan smiled. It was a good choice.

Eventually, after nearly half an hour, Ryan saw Ben come out, stuff a file into his bag and leave.

Then Ryan went to Steve's office and knocked.

'Come in.' Steve's voice.

'Can I –' Ryan began to ask.

'Hello, Ryan,' Steve said, half standing. 'Come in. What's up?'

Ryan had something to talk to Steve about. That was what he was here for.

'There's a problem on the team,' Ryan said, without hesitating.

'OK.'

'I know why Craig is being like he is.'

'I see.' Steve was leaning towards Ryan now.

'His dad's in prison,' Ryan said.

Steve sat back down.

Ryan studied his face. He actually looked sad. Like he'd heard some really bad news about his own family.

'That's terrible,' Steve said. 'Poor lad.'

Ryan said nothing more. He didn't really know what to say. He had his idea – a way of trying to help Craig – but he wanted to see if Steve had something better to say. Steve was the manager, after all.

But Steve said nothing. There was a silence between them.

Eventually Steve said, 'What do you think we should do?'

Ryan was surprised. Steve was asking his opinion. This was the time to bring it up.

'You know Neil Kelly?'

'I do.'

'What if he were to talk to Craig?' Ryan said. He had worried that as soon as he started saying what he thought to Steve, it'd sound stupid. But it didn't. So he carried on. 'What if he could help?'

Steve stood up.

'That is a great idea, Ryan. I know Neil. I can talk to him. Yes. Yes, that's it!'

Steve sounded excited.

'Will you do it, then?' Ryan asked.

'I will. I'll give Neil a call now. Go round and see him. Maybe tonight. That's such a good idea, Ryan. Thank you for telling me. I'm proud of you, son.'

The Boss

Leaving Steve's office, Ryan walked across the courtyard towards the car park. There were still a couple of TV camera teams there. Plus what must have been other journalists and photographers standing around waiting to see if they could get an interview with the new first-team manager.

Ryan walked through the car park and headed for the road that used to be the very long drive leading to the old house. As he did he saw a man climbing out of a car.

Ryan looked again. He seemed familiar. He was tall and athletic but balding. Otherwise he looked like the player he had been ten years before.

'Hello, son,' the man said. 'Are you a United fan?'

Ryan realized who he was. The new manager. Martyn Bedford.

For a second he was tongue-tied.

'Er . . . no. I mean yes. I'm a player too.'

'A player?' Bedford smiled. 'Well, I'm the new boss.'

'I mean for the under-twelves,' Ryan said, smiling now. 'I'm the captain.'

Bedford stopped and shook Ryan's hand.

Ryan had always thought it felt funny – an adult shaking his hand. But it was pretty good that it was the new United manager who was doing it.

'And you're a United fan too?'

'All my life,' Ryan said proudly.

'And do you and the other under-twelves get to see United much? The first team? When they play on Saturdays. I think you play on Sundays, don't you?'

'We do,' Ryan said, aware that some of the photographers he'd seen in the courtyard had approached them and were taking photos of Bedford and him talking. 'I mean, we do play on Sundays. But I don't get to watch United much. It's too expensive and my mum . . .'

As Ryan was explaining, the first-team manager pulled out an envelope.

'They gave me fifteen tickets for the City match on Saturday. To hand out. You know?'

Ryan nodded. He was hoping Bedford was going to give him one of them. He'd been dying to see United all season, but his mum always said that they didn't have any spare money.

Bedford handed him the whole envelope. 'How about you get all your team-mates to come along on Saturday? We could use your support.'

Ryan beamed. He couldn't believe it.

'Listen, son,' the manager said, gesturing towards the journalists who were waiting a few metres away. 'I need to talk to this lot. But I'll see you there on Saturday. And make sure you sing your hearts out.'

'We will,' Ryan said. 'Thank you. Thank you!'

'You're welcome, son.'

And with that the new first-team manager headed towards the TV cameras and the journalists. Ryan heard the first questions that were thrown at him.

'Do you think you can keep United up?'

'Have you met the players yet?'

'Will you be bringing in a new coaching staff – or will you stick with the existing set-up?'

Ryan headed off down the drive. He felt good. He was going to see United for the first time this season. And he had tickets to hand out to the rest of the team. He couldn't wait to tell them!

The First Team

Two days later, Ryan was standing with most of his team-mates to cheer the United first team as they came out on to the pitch.

The noise was brilliant. That's what Ryan always loved about going to a match. The noise. The fans singing and chanting. Not a spare seat in the stadium.

And he couldn't help thinking that one day this could be him – he could be running out to all this noise. A first-team player.

He smiled. At least then no one would be able to hear his mum and all her shouting.

Ryan was sitting next to Ben. Along from them were Chi, Will and Tony. Then Craig. All supporting United. And on the end, Tomasz and Jake, both City fans. Sam, Yunis and Daniel hadn't been able to make it.

Ben was taking the mickey out of Ryan, who was pictured in a national paper talking to Martyn Bedford, under the caption '*Bedford gets to know the United fan base*'.

Steve had insisted on coming along. Ryan knew why. They were his team; he wanted to make sure they behaved themselves.

'Thanks for this, Ryan,' Chi shouted above the noise of the crowd. 'I can't believe you managed to get these tickets!'

'It was luck,' Ryan said.

'Well, cheers, anyway.'

The match kicked off.

United – who had been playing badly all season – started well and were passing the ball quickly to feet. Ryan was glad to see that Neil Kelly was playing. He wondered if Steve had managed to have a word with him yet.

After twenty-two minutes the first goal went in. City were attacking down the left and had fired in a cross. But United's centre back intercepted it and suddenly United were on the attack. It was three against two.

Two passes and United's main striker was one-on-one with the keeper. He touched it twice, then fired it into the net.

One–nil.

The noise was deafening.

It was as if the United fans were letting out all the frustration of the disappointing season at once. The United fans were on their feet jumping around, hugging each other.

Except Tomasz and Jake. They were staring at the pitch, looking furious.

Ryan decided to leave them alone.
He could take the mickey now, but if City
equalized they'd be able to take the mickey
out of *him*.

At half-time United were still one up.

Steve gestured to Ryan.

'Come with me to get some drinks for the
lads,' he said.

The rest of the under-twelves team stayed
in the stand. There was a penalty competition
happening on the pitch, between the United
and City mascots. It was two–nil to City.
Ryan didn't want to stay and watch the City
mascot win.

As they queued at the shop, Steve talked.

'I've got us into the players' lounge
afterwards.'

'What?' Ryan couldn't believe it.

'The lads. You and me. In the players'

lounge,' Steve said. 'I wanted to get Craig to meet Neil. Do you think it's a good idea?'

Ryan was amazed. First that he was going to be in the players' lounge after a match. Second that Steve was asking his opinion about something so important. Again.

'I think it's a great idea,' he said. 'A brilliant idea.'

Second Half

The second half was tense on the pitch. United were desperate for their first win in six weeks. City were trying to score, but without giving too much away at the back.

And it was even more tense in the stands.

Ryan was sitting with his hands squeezed between his knees. Every time City attacked he felt his heart leap into his mouth. He kept looking at Jake and Tomasz, who were leaning forward, but saying nothing.

Ryan really wanted United to win this.
If they got three points they'd be out of
the relegation zone. And the team would
be feeling more confident. If they let in an
equalizer – and results went against them
– then they could be bottom of the league
tonight.

And try as he might to focus on the game,
he couldn't stop worrying about his mum.
She'd not been to see Steve. But he knew
Steve was going to talk to her. Tomorrow,
probably.

But he was at the match, so he tried
to forget about it and concentrate on
United.

With five minutes to go, the unthinkable
happened.

City were attacking more and more. And,
at the end of a good move, their striker broke
free into the penalty area. A United defender
lunged in to tackle. The striker fell. And the
referee pointed to the penalty spot.

Suddenly, everyone was on their feet.

'He dived!'

'No way!'

Everyone was shouting at once. Men's voices. Loud and aggressive.

And for the first time that day you could hear the City fans.

Ryan looked across at Jake and Tomasz. They were sitting in exactly the same position they had been all along. Leaning forward. But Ryan could detect a slight smile on Jake's face.

The City striker took the ball into his hands. He placed it on the penalty spot.

The atmosphere had gone quiet. As if everyone was breathing in. Ready to cheer. Or shout more abuse at the referee.

Ryan looked at Jake and Tomasz again. He saw Tomasz with his hands together, as if he was praying.

The striker took two steps backwards, then ran at the ball.

Behind the goal the United fans were jeering and waving their arms and scarves in the air.

The striker hit the ball. Low and hard. Towards the bottom left corner.

There was a thud. Then another thud.

Ryan wasn't sure what had happened. Until he saw the ball was back in play.

It had hit the post.

And everyone was on their feet cheering.

Except Jake and Tomasz, who were still seated, leaning forward, as if nothing had happened.

Five minutes later the referee blew the final whistle.

The noise from the crowd was deafening.

United 1 City 0.

Then they started chanting the new manager's name:

One Martyn Bedford
There's only one Martyn Bedford

The manager waved to the crowd and shook the hands of the City manager and some of his players.

Then he jogged up to the front of the stand where the under-twelves were sitting. And he put his thumbs up. To Ryan.

Ryan put his thumb up too. Then he looked at Steve.

'Did he just put his thumbs up at us?' Ryan said.

'He did,' Steve said. 'At you.'

Neil Kelly

R yan led the rest of the under-twelves into the players' lounge.

The first things he noticed were pictures of great players from the past. Players holding trophies. Players scoring famous goals. All pictures he had in his United books at home.

One day there would be a picture of him on the wall in this room. That's what he wanted. That was his dream.

But today, Ryan remembered, was not about him. It was about Craig.

Steve was hoping to get Neil Kelly to talk to Craig about his dad being in prison. Craig must be going through a really hard time. And Kelly might be able to help him open up.

The under-twelves sat together at a long table that had been set out for them. There were two large jugs of juice and some food: chocolate biscuits, sausage rolls. Ryan felt a bit embarrassed. It looked like a children's party in the middle of the adult players' lounge.

Craig was feeling different.

Although he couldn't say it to anyone, this was nice. Really nice. And the best thing was he'd be able to tell his dad about it.

When he'd gone to prison to visit his dad, he'd been so nervous about being there, he hadn't known what he should say.

But now he had this.

His dad was a massive United fan. He'd been to hundreds of games. He worshipped the players. And he'd be so proud to see his son here in the players' lounge after beating City one–nil.

Craig saw Ryan looking at him. He looked back.

'You OK?' Ryan asked.

Craig nodded. He knew Ryan had got them the tickets for this game. But he just couldn't bring himself to say thank you. Ryan was all right; even though he was captain, it didn't mean he was anything special.

Craig saw Ryan staring behind him. He turned round to see what he was looking at.

The players had arrived. They were shaking hands with older men. Holding drinks. Laughing.

Craig recognized City players too.

He looked at Jake. He wanted to tell Jake that they'd arrived. But something stopped him doing that too. And even though he was surrounded by all these people, he felt lonely.

Then he saw Steve coming towards the under-twelves. With someone else.

Neil Kelly.

And they were heading straight for Craig.

Brotherly Love

'This is Craig,' Steve said.

'Hello, Craig,' Kelly said. 'Did you enjoy the game?'

Steve had led Craig and Kelly away to a table out of earshot of the rest of the lads and the players.

Craig knew what was going on. He knew Kelly's brother was in prison. He knew what Steve was up to: have Kelly talk to him to help him. He didn't know how Steve had found out, but he supposed everybody knew his dad was in prison now.

But he didn't mind. He'd never spoken to a first-team player before. He felt good sitting at a table with a Premier League player. Talking one to one.

'Steve tells me your dad's in prison,' Kelly said.

'Yeah,' Craig said, nodding. 'For six months.'

'Are you close?'

'Yeah.' Craig felt a wave of sadness wash over him. But he tried not to think about it. He was afraid he'd cry.

'Me too,' said the player. 'My brother would have loved to have seen this game. He hates City. He used to come in here with me after all the games.'

Now Kelly looked sad. Craig felt like saying something to make him feel better. But what do you say to a Premier League player who feels sad? What can you do to make him feel better?

'I'm sorry,' Craig said.

'Thanks, Craig,' Kelly said.

For a moment there was silence between them.

Then Kelly spoke. 'I find it really hard. He's never missed a game with me playing at United. I always knew he was in the crowd.' Kelly looked surprised at the thought.

'My dad's not missed any either,' Craig
said.

'No?'

'No.'

Craig felt really strange. It was nice
talking to this man. They had things in
common.

'Have you been to visit him?' Kelly said.
'Your dad?'

'Last week,' Craig said.

'What was it like?'

Craig shrugged. 'I don't know. We didn't say much to each other. And I was a bit nervous.'

'I'm going tomorrow,' the player smiled. 'I'm nervous.'

Craig looked at Kelly. Would he really be nervous visiting his brother in prison? A grown man.

'Are you?' Craig asked.

'I am. I don't know what to expect.'

So Craig told him. Led him up the path, through the doors, up to the desk and into the waiting area.

Kelly nodded as he spoke. Like he was really listening. Like he really wanted to hear what Craig had to say.

When Craig had finished they shared another silence. Kelly breathed in and let out a deep sigh. And Craig realized he really was nervous.

But Craig could also see there were other people waiting to talk to the player.

'I think they want to talk to you too,' he said, nodding in their direction.

'They always do,' Kelly said. 'You'll find that when you're in the first team.'

Craig grinned.

Kelly went on. 'Have you got a game this weekend?'

'Tomorrow. We've got Huddersfield at home.'

Kelly nodded. 'Well, good luck,' he said. 'Thanks for talking to me.'

Craig wondered what he meant. Why was he thanking him? *It should be the other way round*, he thought.

Make or Break

Craig felt better for the next game. His three-match suspension for the sending-off the week before wasn't due to start until the next week, so he was able to play.

But he knew it was because Steve had no other choice, with so many players missing.

There *were* new players on the bench, though. Two lads from the under-elevens who had been doing well. But neither of them were in the starting line-up. Steve was also scouting for a couple of new players too – players he could trial in the second half of the season.

Craig wanted to try hard. He wanted to play a game without getting into trouble. Without losing his temper.

With all these new players coming in, his place on the team – even in the squad – might be under threat.

Huddersfield were good. And very physical. They were happy to challenge for every ball. And happy to foul too.

Craig had already heard Ryan's mum shouting at the referee, that he should keep more control of the game.

After ten minutes Huddersfield scored. And Craig knew he was partly to blame. He'd moved up the field to win the ball and left a gap behind him. A gap Ryan and Tony couldn't fill.

Nil–one.

The problem for Craig was the winger coming down Huddersfield's right-hand side. He was quick. Too quick. Craig was having trouble having any impact on the game.

Every time the ball came down the right, the winger beat Craig. And every time that happened Craig felt more and more unhappy.

He was starting to have that feeling again. Anger. Frustration. He didn't know what you were meant to call it. But he knew how to get rid of it.

He'd hack the winger down, then he'd not be so fast. Craig might pick up a booking, but so what? He was going to miss the next three games anyway. And the ref wasn't booking the Huddersfield players for their dirty play.

That was it. The next time the winger came at him Craig would let him have it.

But then he heard something.

'Come on, Craig. Just keep with him.'

It sounded like his dad. Or the sort of thing his dad would say. Craig looked up, knowing it couldn't be his dad.

And then he saw. Standing next to Jake's dad – Neil Kelly.

Craig couldn't believe it.

The player had come to see *him*. This was amazing.

At half-time, Steve let Kelly have a word with the lads. To help with his team talk.

It was one all now. Jake had scored an equalizer just minutes before.

'I thought you were great,' Kelly said. 'The way you came back from one down, that showed character. You can win this.'

Steve nodded and thanked the player. Then he ushered the under-twelves on to the pitch. Bringing off Tony and Sam, replacing them with two of the under-elevens, Ben Hansford and Imran.

Ryan led the team back on, talking to the new players, helping them to settle in.

And as he did, he saw his mum and Steve talking. He could only see Steve's face. His mum had turned away from him.

Steve looked serious.

Ryan wondered what he was saying. And what the repercussions would be for him.

But he had to put that out of his mind now. He had a game to play. That had to be his focus.

Craig was happy to be still in the game.

He heard Kelly shout to him as they went back on: 'Keep on at that winger. You've got him now. He knows he can't beat you.'

Craig smiled and ran on to the pitch. He felt good. It was a bit like having his dad on the pitchside again. Someone encouraging him. Someone watching him, making sure he was doing the right things.

Now he was going to show just how well he could play for United.

Craig's Back

The second half went well. And Ryan was really happy how things were going. On the pitch, anyway.

First, the new centre back, Imran, was amazing. Ryan could tell immediately that he was a stronger player than Tony.

Since James had retired, the defence had been all over the place, but this was better. The best thing was he trusted Imran to deal with the Huddersfield players.

Also, Craig was doing well.

Something had changed. It was like the old Craig was back. Every time Huddersfield attacked, Craig was in the right place. The winger, who had been tormenting him during the first half, just couldn't get past him now.

The winning goal came midway into the second half.

United were attacking, Ben racing down the wing with the ball when he was tackled. Huddersfield regained possession quickly and fired the ball across the field to the winger who had been troubling Craig. This time Craig was out of position. And the winger was running freely into United's half.

But he didn't see Craig's run. Craig had never run so fast. He was determined not to let the winger beat him.

So he ran up behind him. Then he lunged, throwing himself at the winger.

Except he didn't catch the winger. He caught the ball. Then he stood up and played an inch-perfect pass to Jake.

Jake ran twenty yards then fired the ball into Yunis. A move they'd done a hundred times.

But this time Yunis dummied the ball, leaving Will a space behind the defenders who were trying to get to Yunis.

It left Will with an easy tap in.

Goal.

Two–one to United.

And what a goal!

'That was amazing!' Kelly said to Craig as he joined the players coming jubilantly out of the dressing rooms.

'Thanks,' Craig said.

'That tackle. You won the game. I'd have been proud of a tackle like that.'

Craig grinned. He remembered how his dad would walk him back to the car after a game. Do his pep talk. He knew his dad wouldn't mind being replaced by Kelly just this once.

'I think the way you gave yourself a bit more time and space to deal with him changed it. It meant you had choices. And he wasn't just beating you with his early pace.'

Craig nodded. Kelly was right.

'Listen,' Kelly said. 'I enjoyed seeing you in the players' lounge yesterday. How about you use my brother's season ticket for the rest of the season?'

'What?' Craig had to stop walking.

'You could have my brother's season ticket. He's not going to be using it. How about it? Then you can come into the players' lounge. We could talk about our prisoners.'

Craig couldn't believe it.

'And you could give me some tips on my game,' Kelly said, grinning.

Behind Craig and Kelly, Ryan was walking with Steve, carrying the sack of balls.

Steve nodded. 'You've done well, Ryan.'

'You too,' Ryan said.

'But you. These last few weeks, you've been a fantastic captain. I'm ever so proud of you. Well done.'

Ryan grinned the widest grin possible.

Then Steve gestured behind him. His mum was walking, head down, slowly. As if she didn't want to be seen.

That was about as unlike Ryan's mum as she could be.

Ryan dropped back. His mum smiled at him. Then frowned. Ryan thought she looked confused.

'Steve told me what he thinks of me,' she said, like a child who has been scolded.

'What –'

'What did he say?' she interrupted.

'Yeah.'

'Just what you told me, Ryan.'

'I'm sorry,' Ryan said.

His mum nodded. 'Maybe *I* should be sorry. I just . . . I just get so . . . involved.'

'I like it,' Ryan said. 'Sometimes.'

'Yeah, well, maybe I should shut up more.'

Then Ryan's mum put her arm round her son, squeezed his shoulder, sighed, and the two of them took up the rear. United's under-twelves, their parents and their coaches walked back to the dressing rooms, happy to be back in winning ways.

Sunday 15 January
United 2 Huddersfield 1
Goals: Jake, Will
Bookings: none

Under-twelves manager's marks out of ten for each player:

Tomasz	7
Daniel	6
Tony (subbed for Imran, half-time)	5
Ryan	7
Craig	8
Chi	6
Jake	8
Yunis	8
Sam (subbed for Ben H, half-time)	6
Ben	6
Will	8
Ben H	6
Imran	8

Thank Yous

My wife is the first person to read all my
books. She helps me get things right before
I show it to anyone else. She has great ideas.
She spots my errors and weaknesses. She
always deserves the biggest thank you. And
– along with my daughter – she gives me the
support and encouragement and self-belief I
need to write books.

Sophie Hannah and James Nash are the
other members of the writing group I am in.
They are both great writers and help me get

the book into shape. Sophie Hannah writes great crime novels and poems, published by Hodder, Penguin, Carcanet and others. James Nash is a great poet and short-story writer, published by several publishers. This book is dedicated to them because I think, without them, I would not have developed as much as I needed to be published by Puffin Books.

Thanks, as always, to Burnley FC for allowing me to spend time at their training ground and get some of the facts about academy football straight. I am thrilled to see them in the Premier League. They are a great club who do a lot in their community among the Pennines.

I'd like to thank everyone at Puffin for the wonderful work they do to make the books look and read so well – and to reach so many people.

Thanks to all the bookshops and libraries

who are supporting this series. Particularly Sonia Benster and her colleagues at The Children's Bookshop in Huddersfield, and Amelia and her colleagues at Madeleine Lindley's in Oldham.

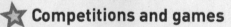

Bright and shiny and sizzling with fun stuff . . .

puffin.co.uk

WEB CHAT

Discover something new
EVERY month – books, competitions
and treats galore

WEB NEWS

The **Puffin Blog** is packed with posts and photos from
Puffin HQ and special guest bloggers. You can also sign up
to our monthly newsletter **Puffin Beak Speak**

WEB FUN

Take a sneaky peek around your favourite **author's studio**,
tune in to the **podcast**, **download activities** and much more

WEBBED FEET

(Puffins have funny little feet and
brightly coloured beaks)

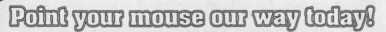

Point your mouse our way today!

It all started with a Scarecrow

Puffin is well over sixty years old.
Sounds ancient, doesn't it? But Puffin has never been
so lively. We're always on the lookout for the next big
idea, which is how it began all those years ago.

Penguin Books was a big idea from the mind of
a man called Allen Lane, who in 1935 invented
the quality paperback and changed the world.
**And from great Penguins, great Puffins grew,
changing the face of children's books forever.**

The first four Puffin Picture Books were hatched in 1940 and the
first Puffin story book featured a man with broomstick arms called
Worzel Gummidge. In 1967 Kaye Webb, Puffin Editor, started the
Puffin Club, promising to **'make children into readers'**.
She kept that promise and over 200,000 children became
devoted Puffineers through their quarterly instalments of
Puffin Post, which is now back for a new generation.

Many years from now, we hope you'll look back and
remember Puffin with a smile. **No matter what your age
or what you're into, there's a Puffin for everyone.**
The possibilities are endless, but one thing is for sure:
whether it's a picture book or a paperback, a sticker book
or a hardback, **if it's got that little Puffin
on it – it's bound to be good.**